For Bruce, with love.
— J. Y.

For Sandra, with love.
— B. M.

Jane Yolen

Sky Dogs

Illustrated by Barry Moser

Harcourt Brace Jovanovich, Publishers

San Diego • New York • London

Requests for permission to make copies of any part of the work
should be mailed to: Permissions Department,
Harcourt Brace Jovanovich, Publishers, Orlando, Florida 32887.

Library of Congress Cataloging-in-Publication Data
Yolen, Jane.
Sky dogs/by Jane Yolen; illustrated by Barry Moser.
p.   cm.
Summary: A young motherless boy in a tribe of Blackfeet Indians
is present when his people see horses for the first time
and are changed forever.
ISBN 0-15-275480-6
ISBN 0-15-275481-4 (ltd. ed.)
1. Siksika Indians — Juvenile fiction. [1. Siksika Indians — Fiction.
2. Indians of North America — Fiction. 3. Horses — Fiction.]
I. Moser, Barry, ill. II. Title.
PZ7.Y78Sk   1990
[E] — dc20   89-26960

Printed in the United States of America

C D E

SKY DOGS

My children, you ask how I came to be called He-who-loves-horses, for now I sit in the tipi, and food is brought to me, and I do not ride the wind. Come close — there, there. Come close, and I will tell you.

Once the land winded us, for we had to walk on our own legs from camp to camp, from sky to sky, with only small dogs to carry our rawhide bags and pull the travois sleds.

The grass beneath our feet sang *swee-swash, swee-swash,*

and we wore out many moccasins along the paths of the plains.

Then one day we saw strange beasts, coming from west of the mountains, coming from Old Man's sleeping room.

They were so far away, we first thought they were long shadows. But the sun was high, and still they came toward us, and that is not how a shadow acts.

Then we saw they were big as elk, with tails of straw. Two Kutani clung to their backs, feet hanging down, like men who have the sickness. And one beast pulled a heavily laden travois, like a big dog.

Then we were afraid.

Jumps-over-the-water, who was my best friend and was born in the same season, hid behind his mother's skirt. And Running Bear, the bravest of us then, born a season sooner, ran behind the nearest tipi. I stood apart and watched with big eyes, not because I was *not* afraid, but because I could not move, because I had been caught out beyond the safety of my father's tipi, beyond the safety of his arms. Often it was so with me since my mother died.

The men of our tribe made the mutterings men make when they want to say: "We are not afraid. No. Not us. We are mighty Piegan. We are warriors of the plains. We drove out the Kutani and took their lands. We rule the wide grass from sky to sky."

But they *were* afraid. Their eyes grew big, and four of them reached out for their hunting bows.

That is because one may fear what comes from Old Man yet not be afraid of any other thing.

Then Long Arrow, our chief, held up his hands and laughed.

"These are from the sky," he said. "These are from out of the hill. I have heard of them. They are called Sky Dogs, a gift from Old Man, like the buffalo, like the antelope, like the bighorn sheep."

Long Arrow knew many things, many tales, for he had walked the world seven times around, from the Porcupine Hills down to the mouth of the Yellowstone, all the world first made by Old Man.

So the mutterings stopped, though three men kept their bows nearby.

And when the newest baby cried out for his supper, I felt something inside me cry out, too. And I was glad when his mother sang softly to him, for then I could listen to the words of his cradleboard song, and they comforted me.

So we waited for the Sky Dogs to reach our camp. But we did not go out to greet them. We did not make a moccasin path to our tipis. We waited the way strong men wait, with

the sacred herb, *nawak'osis*, ready for smoking and the meat of buffalo on the fire.

But three warriors kept their faces toward the west, for to be strong does not mean you sleep, does not mean you turn away from danger.

When they arrived at last, there were three Kutani, not two: a woman lying sick on the travois and two men slung on the Sky Dogs' backs like rawhide carrying bags.

We took them in, but they were too ill to share our feast. And the men died in Long Arrow's tipi before nightfall, before they could tell us all about the Sky Dogs, before they could sing the praises of Old Man, who gave such a gift.

We fed the beasts dried meat like any dogs. We rubbed their noses with good backfat, which made them sneeze. We threw sticks before their faces so they could run and bring the sticks back. But they were startled by the throwing sticks, and one Sky Dog ran away. We did not see it again.

Long Arrow said it went to Old Man's house, that Old Man had called it home — though someone else said a coyote or wolf would catch it first, and the women laughed, like running water, behind their hands.

But two of them remained, dogs as big as elk. They turned from us and put their faces into the prairie grass, eating loudly so we would know how to feed them.

Running Bear came out from behind the tipi.

Jumps-over-the-water left his mother's skirt.

And I — I touched the back leg of the smallest Sky Dog, running my hand up as high as it would go. His skin was soft and warm, and he crunched the grass with sounds as loud as a careless man walking: *snick-snack, snick-snack*. In this way I knew he was not afraid. I knew he would not run back

to Old Man's house or into the teeth of coyote or wolf.

I leaned my cheek against his flank. He smelled like the plains after the buffalo have passed by. When I patted his nose, he made a low snorting laugh, and Long Arrow, our chief, smiled at me.

The woman who had been sick grew well, and soon she became my father's wife and my Kutani mother. She sang to me, late into the night, all the Sky Dog songs of her people.

So, it was I who learned first, of all the Piegan, how to run the bone comb through the Sky Dog's forelock; how to blow into his nostrils to make him follow; how to twist my fingers in his mane and pull myself onto his back; how to ride into battle and count swift coup.

That is why, my children, I am called He-who-loves-horses. That is how I earned my own place in the council of warriors.

And that is how the great Piegan, the people of many horses, became masters of the plains. So it is pictured there on the trade cloth, so it is painted there on my tipi, so it is recorded here, here in my heart, all my children.

AUTHOR'S NOTE

There are several legends about the coming of the horse to the Blackfeet, of which the Piegan are a band. Some of the stories are magical and full of mythic elements in which Elk Dogs or Sky Dogs or Spirit Dogs are brought back by a hero (sometimes named Long Arrow) from a land under water.

Other, more realistic stories mention how some Kutani (or Kootenay), members of a tribe defeated years before by the Blackfeet, accidentally wandered into a Piegan village riding on strange, alien creatures. These creatures of legend were horses. Before the time of horses, the Plains Indians had used camp dogs to carry bundles or pull the travois sled when they traveled from camp to camp. Once they had horses, life changed for the Blackfeet people, for they could cut their hunting time and go great distances to raid and trade.

I have drawn from parts of these stories as well as parts of tales about the Blackfeet creator, Old Man, to make a new story about a small, motherless Piegan boy who was part of the band that first had horses.

Nawak'osis, the sacred herb, is what we call tobacco. *Backfat*, a grease, comes from the hump of the buffalo. To *count coup* a warrior touches his enemy with his hand or a coup stick without causing physical hurt — an honor for the warrior, a disgrace for the enemy.

While horses made a great difference to the Blackfeet, white men made a much greater one. When they first arrived, the white men were greeted by the Blackfeet, who traded goods for guns, and for knives with which to skin trade animals, and for white blankets, which the young men favored, and for black coats for the old men. But all too soon white men killed off the buffalo, causing many hundreds of Blackfeet to starve. Finally they forced the Blackfeet, like other Native American tribes, onto restricted areas of land, called "reservations." The Blackfeet warrior Flint Knife said, "I wish that white people had never come into my country."